Echoes From The Mountains

Selected Poems of Ghani Khan

Translated by

Dr. Khalida Nasim

2024

Copyright

Published in 2024 by Green Zone Publishing
A division of Dr. Sohail MPC Inc.
213 Byron St. South
Whitby, Ontario Canada L1N 4P7
T. 905-666-7253   F. 905-666-4397

Dr. Khalida Nasim
Echoes From The Mountain — Selected Poems of Ghani Khan

ISBN: 978-1-927874-68-4

Cover Design: Shahid Shafiq
Textual Design: Marcelina Naini

Dedicated to my father,

Through whose eyes,

I learned to fill the canvas of life with color.

Ghani Khan (1914 - 1996)

ECHOES FROM THE MOUNTAINS

Sitting on the balcony,

I look at the mountains,

Standing tall,

With peaks in the sky

Decorated with emerald green trees,

A sprinkle of light rain

Touches my face,

The delicate breeze

Caresses my skin,

I am envious,

The beauty is so vast,

My greed takes it all in,

The mountains,
Speak to me,

Echoing!!

Is this Poetry?

The words reach out,

Hold my hand,

And take me along,

I walk with them,

The mountains,
The beauty,
The words, and I,
All become one,
All one poetry

      ~ Khalida Nasim

Table of Contents

ACKNOWLEDGMENTS

I am deeply thankful to all those who contributed to this project and helped make it a reality. I am especially grateful to my beloved friend and mentor, Dr. Khalid Sohail, for his valuable input and encouragement. He always believed in my abilities more than myself.

I want to recognize the support of my dearest friend, Dr. Kamran Ahmed, for his constant encouragement and advice.

I appreciate Professor Tasbihullah very much. He was a source of clarification whenever I struggled to understand any verse. He is like an ocean of knowledge in Ghani Khan's poetry.

I greatly admire Arthur Skip Maselli, a friend, poet, and a great Sufi. His poetic sense and wisdom were a valuable source of guidance for me.

Thanks to my writer friend, Mr. Naeem Ashraf, for his poetry review and acknowledgment. His keen interest and friendly push were added forces to make this book a reality.

I extend my humble gratitude to Ghani Khan's beloved family. Thank you for welcoming me into your home. You re-ignited my inspiration for Ghani Khan's poetry by allowing me to revisit old memories.

I want to recognize the support of Mr. Aziz Khan from Nandara channel, Peshawar, KPK, for helping find useful resources whenever needed.

I am indebted to Mr. Shahid Shafiq, who put his heart into the creation of the title page. His artistic sense was the best way to give the book a face.

Thanks to Marcelina at Green Zone Publications for her review and input.

Most importantly, a big thanks to my children, who were my first audience at every step of my translations and, with their young minds and knowledge, contributed valuable insights. Their love for our Pashtun culture and language is both a comfort and an inspiration. I relied heavily on their knowledge of technology throughout this project. I love you very much.

GHANI KHAN — A POET PHILOSOPHER OF PAKISTAN BY: KHALID SOHAIL

I thank Dr. Khalida Nasim for introducing me and many other poetry lovers to the mystery and magic of Ghani Khan's poetry.

I have known Khalida for more than a decade. When I first met her, I was pleasantly surprised to learn that she had graduated from Khyber Medical College in Peshawar, Pakistan, the same medical college I had graduated from a few years earlier. I was further surprised to discover that her house in Pakistan was not only in the same city but also on the same Charsadda Road, a couple of miles from my house. We lived in the same neighbourhood, not knowing that we would meet decades later in Toronto, thousands of miles from our homes.

I found it amazing and inspiring that Khalida travelled hundreds of miles to attend literary meetings of Family of the Heart, an informal group of artists and journalists, poets and philosophers, writers and scholars of Toronto. As time passed and our friendship strengthened, I was delighted to learn that Khalida was a very well-read writer and doctor with a keen interest in a wide range of topics, including literature and philosophy, psychology and spirituality.

I was impressed and delighted to find out that Khalida was translating Pashto poet Ghani Khan's poems into English. What a wonderful literary gift to English-speaking readers, I thought. I believe that translators are the stepchildren of literature as they are not given as much recognition and respect as they deserve. In my humble opinion translators are those special and unique writers who build literary bridges between two languages and traditions, communities and cultures.

As a humanist psychotherapist, when I reflect on my literary and philosophical journey, I realize that I would not have benefited from the writings of Sigmund Freud and Carl Jung, Karl Marx and Mao Tse-Tung, Jalal ud din, Rumi and Khalil Gibran, Frantz Kafka and Pablo Neruda, had their masterpieces not been translated. It is because of those translations of the world's literature that we have become members of a global village.

Khalida's translations of Ghani Khan's poems build a creative bridge between the East and the West, Pakistan and Canada, Pushto and English. I feel fortunate to have the pleasure and honour of reading them before they are published in the form of a book.

When we study Ghani Khan's biography and poetry, we realize that he was not only a poet, but also a philosopher. He was a brave man who stood firm in what he believed and made sacrifices for his ideas and ideals. He was even jailed for his social and political commitments.

When I read Ghani Khan's poems, I realized that he was aware of many of life's secrets. He expressed his deep insights in his poems. Let me share some of his poetic and philosophical ideas that impressed me, as they might inspire you to study him more seriously.

In spite of life's struggles and challenges, Ghani Khan never gives up. Even in humanity's darkest nights, he is hopeful that we will one day see dawn. He writes:

A day in summer,

Like a long winter night,

A silence,

A stillness all over,

Somewhere faraway,

A spark,

Of light,

A star?

Or a faraway desert's fire,

Tells me,

In small words,

If the mountain is big,

It has a path to the top

Ghani Khan's poetry has the innocence of a child. He is full of curiosity about life. He asks,

How can I fit

The earth and the sky,

In just a little corner?

And how can I capture

An ocean,

In a single dew drop?

Alongside a child's innocence, Ghani Khan's poems also have the wisdom of an older man. He shares his insight in these words,

When I gave away my garden,

Only then it became mine

I learned to fly high

When in fire I burnt my wings to fly

Alongside a child's innocence and an older man's wisdom, Ghani Khan's poems also contain the passion of youth. That passion is reflected in love, the biggest and profoundest secret of life. Ghani Khan says,

A heart without love,

Like a withered flower,

With love, it is a spark of light

Without love, it's like a handful of dust

I would like to thank Dr. Khalida Nasim for introducing the world to Ghani Khan, a poet and philosopher of Pakistan and sharing his deep love and profound wisdom by translating his Pushto poems into English.

I feel a sense of pride being Dr. Khalida Nasim's friend and a co-traveller on her literary journey. I wish her all the best in her personal, professional, and philosophical journey. I hope that this book is the first drop of rain and that she will one day publish her own poems and stories. I am always impressed by her honesty and sincerity, humility and integrity. We need more Khalida Nasims and Ghani Khans to create a just and peaceful world. Like her hero, Ghani Khan, Khalida Nasim also has a heart of gold.

Khalida Nasim's translations have become a creative bridge between Ghani Khan and the world. I would like to congratulate her for her hard work and tireless efforts. Such commitment and dedication are rare, very rare, these days.

ECHOES... FROM THE POET TO THE AUTHOR AND BEYOND...
BY: DR. KAMRAN AHMAD

Dr. Khalida Nasim, in her youth, did not only sit, talk, and eat with Ghani Khan. It was an initiation. Since then, she has been on a journey, with the seed of his spirit that got planted into her, continuing to grow. She is still on that journey of growing into him. And that is the journey that her book invites us on as well. To allow him, the archetypal force that he is, to take root and spread his magic within us. To transform our psyche with his mystical vision. To transform us... as individuals, as communities, and as nations.

Dr. Khalida Nasim took her first breath in the air which gave Ghani Khan his voice. She took root in the soil that gave form to Ghani Khan. That air and that soil they both remained lovingly connected to.

But they also share the courage that the land is known for. This courage allows them, in addition to loving that land and the traditions of that land, to challenge the parts of these

traditions that need to be challenged. They share
the courage to shape aspects of their lives in ways
that are radically different from the traditions.
How he did that right through his life and
relationships, you will read about in the book.
Her... I saw her doing 24-hour shifts at the
hospital, then travelling off to faraway places
alone and at other times, playing her sitar, sitting
comfortably in her home, overlooking a
picturesque lake. Their lives, therefore, become
an inspiration for others, both men and women,
to continue transforming their lives and their
culture as a living conversation.

Their land, Khyber Pakhtunkhwa, the
country, and the whole of South Asia today are
struggling with rigidity and extremism in
religion. The spirit of Ghani Khan that Dr.
Khalida Nasim gives us access to is needed today
even more than when Ghani Khan gave voice to
it. The timeless truths in his verses are more
relevant today than when Ghani Khan put them
into words. These truths and this spirit are
relevant and needed today as if our lives depend
on it. For, today, in the whole of the country, our
lives literally do depend on it.

Those who do not know Pushto have had access to Ghani Khan through other translations also. What makes Dr. Khalida Nasim's translations different is that his voice now reaches us through the words, through the eyes, and through the experiences of a woman. She has lived a full life. Over the years, in my conversations with her, I saw the alchemy of the verses as she used them to make sense of her own life. The verses have that power... to transform our vision and our being. I had the honour of witnessing that continued transformation in her.

What Dr. Khalida Nasim brings to us, what she invites us to, is, therefore, a living, breathing, dynamic process of inner transformation. She invites us to step into a larger self, a larger life, and a larger universe.

WALKING INTO POETRY

At around 11 am on a pleasant spring day in March 1988, four classmates and I arrived in Hashtnagar, Charsadda, to visit Ghani Khan at his home for an interview. I was one of the editors of the Pashto section of our medical college magazine, *Cenna*.

Ghani Khan, the esteemed poet of the Pashto language, famously known as *Lewany Falsafi* (mad philosopher), ruled hearts in literary circles and among the common people of KPK and Pakistan. His poetry was especially popular amongst the youth. Like many, I, too, was fond of his poetry. Ghani Khan's poems sung by Sardar Ali Takkar (a legendary Pashtun singer) have been part of my everyday music selection. One such verse read:

"If I am young forever
My youth will become a burden,

I value it much because

It is so short"

I remember the goosebumps that I'd get from listening to these verses. Sardar Ali's enchanting voice seemed created for Ghani Khan's poetry. He perfected the art of bringing Ghani Khan's verses to life through his melodies. The combination of the two would create a masterpiece.

In Hashtnagar, one of Ghani Khan's family members welcomed us at the door of his *hujra*. The *hujra* is integral to Pashtun living, especially in the villages. It serves as a place for people to come together, socialize, and exchange ideas over a cup of tea or a meal.

The entrance to Ghani Khan's *hujra* was a grand arch-like door that took us to an open garden with thick green grass, various big and small trees, and countless flower bushes. A gravelled path took us to the veranda, where *charpais* (a traditional wood lounger) with oversized pillows on one side and chairs on the other were invitingly set up. The man who had greeted us made us comfortable, offered us water to drink, and went inside the house through another grand arch-like doorway to inform Ghani Khan about our arrival. Soon, the man returned and asked us to follow him inside the house.

The house was like a lush dreamland with trees, plants, and flowers everywhere - a place where one could feel Mother Nature in its purest form. The man took us straight to the porch where Ghani Khan, now in his 70s, with peppery gray hair and an inviting soft smile, was sitting on a *charpai*. He was dressed in a gray *shalwar kameez* and gray-black vest. A simple man with an authentic, grand personality and a genuine smile. He greeted us with a fatherly warmth.

At the time of our meeting, it had been only a few months since his only son, Faridoon Khan, had passed away at a young age, merely in his mid-thirties. Despite the weight of this pain, Ghani Khan maintained his composure with a gentle smile. Ghani Khan's close friends said that this man with the strength of a mountain was shaken to his core by his son's passing. This was reflected in his poetry from that time onwards, such as these lines from the poem titled:

A Lost Dream

An adorable child
Perhaps a thought
Or a hangover — -!
With a smile, he peeked
Through the darkness
Of eternity

O' my little boy
Where would you be?

Wandering
Lost in the dark
When your place is in light

Why have you become
A dream lost in eternity
In your beauty is my life
You live in my breath
Like a madman
I am searching everywhere
For a beloved, I lost

Amazingly, throughout our meeting with Ghani Khan, we never sensed any weakness in his demeanour. His son's passing came up briefly in the discussion, and he handled it with complete composure and dignity, swallowing the lump of sorrow in his throat with his known strength. He had a simple way of talking, using everyday language riddled with jokes and funny metaphors. He came across as a simple, strong village man but also gentle and mentally sharp. There was something extraordinary about him that would leave a mark to stay with me for a lifetime.

He gave us signed copies of his poetry collection, *De Ghani Kulyat*, which is a significant part of my most valued possessions.

Our meeting came at the time when his work, like many other progressive writers, faced opposition from religious and political groups such as the *Jamaat-e Islami* and the then-governing forces.

Cenna's Urdu language section editors had interviewed Ahmad Faraz, another legendary Urdu poet who, like Ghani Khan, was part of the progressive writers' group. When the *Jamaat-e-Islami* students in our college found out about these interviews, they incited a raucous protest against its publication. They broke into the principal's office, threatening to cause damage if the interviews were published.

Under such pressure and to maintain peace at the institution, that year's magazine was banned from publication.

Today, Ghani Khan and Ahmed Faraz are the poets most read and loved by poetry lovers.

ECHOES FROM THE MOUNTAINS

After my first meeting with Ghani Khan, I greatly desired to keep coming to him and learn from his wisdom. But life offers its own agenda, which didn't allow me much opportunity to fulfill this desire. I only met him one more time in 1989 when he was admitted to the Lady Reading Hospital in Peshawar for some health-related issues. I was still a medical student at the time. We talked only briefly, as he was frail due to his illness. Afterwards, I moved to Karachi for post-graduation at Aga Khan University Hospital. Life became busy with family, work and other day-to-day struggles. Then, one day in 1996, I heard the news of his passing. The news hit me hard. It felt like a world that I wanted to explore and immerse in perished. Like many of us do, I underestimated the limitations of time. But his poetry never left me. It followed me through the decades as my journey took me from Pakistan to Canada.

In October 2020, I visited Ghani Khan's village, house, and grave. It was a sad moment when, after almost a quarter of a century since I had last seen him, I was standing at his grave, remembering his smiling face and his grace.

I thought of the lines from his poem *Khawray* (Dust),

No, my friend,
Death is not the end of being,
With emptying of the wine cup,
The bliss doesn't end
This strange ocean of being,
Must have an unseen other shore,

In graves are buried,
Hands and feet, lips and fingers,
But who can make a grave?
For the rapture of drunk eyes

And that was true. I could feel Ghani Khan's presence at that moment and whenever I read or listened to his poetry. His rapture is truly alive.

Later that day, I revisited his *hujra* and house. His family, a traditional Pashtun hospitable family, welcomed me with great respect and love. I talked with his family and visited the same room where we had lunch with Ghani Khan when I first met him. I visited his library, where he had kept his paintings and sculpture collections. Everything seemed to be in the same place. The memories of many years back were playing on my mind's screen when Ghani Khan himself had accompanied us to these rooms. He had talked passionately about his work and the feelings behind every piece of his art. Now, 24 years later, his spirit could be felt in the room. His verses echoed to me from decades past. Ghani Khan's poetry took on even more importance for me in his death than in his life.

Through the years, I wanted to share what I saw in his words with my friends. This desire led to the translations for my Urdu and English-speaking friends. This book manifests my sincere love and respect for Ghani Khan. My work will continue as his wisdom remains a part of my life.

A NOTE TO THE READERS

The beauty of a poet's words is in the language, metaphors, and manner of speech they employ. Translating poetry into another language is not an easy task, and it remains true that Ghani Khan's poetry blossoms beautifully through Pashto's eloquence. However, I have tried to the best of my ability to honour that eloquence and to transmit to readers the feelings and the essence of Ghani Khan's poems. To this end, I have taken the liberty to move the words around within the limits of the thought wherever it became necessary. I have also refrained from translating some words from the original language and have instead provided the meaning in footnotes. I took this liberty wherever I felt that the beauty of the word was at risk of being lost if directly translated into English.

The mountains in the title symbolize the grand province of Khyber Pakhtunkhwa (KPK). The magic of these lush mountains is synonymous with the beauty of the Pashto language, especially when used in poetry. I feel like Ghani Khan's words echo through the mountains, and the world can hear them if they are listened to with attention.

INTRODUCTION

Ghani Khan was born in 1914 in Hashtnagar, in the modern-day village of Utmanzai in the Charsadda District of the Khyber Pakhtunkhwa (KPK) province of Pakistan. He was the eldest son of Abdul Ghaffar Khan, famously known as Bacha Khan, a prominent non-violence movement activist during the Indian independence period. Ghani Khan had two brothers who also became distinguished figures in KPK; Abdul Wali Khan continued his father's political movement, and Abdul Ali Khan became an educationist and vice-chancellor of Peshawar University.

The second decade of the 20th century, when Ghani Khan was born, was a time of significant changes in the world. The Ottoman Empire had just collapsed, leading to the formation of many states in the Middle East. The First World War started in 1914, causing the loss of lives, scarcity of basic needs, and growing discontent worldwide. The formation of the Soviet Union as a result of the Bolshevik Revolution of 1917 had its effects on neighbouring countries. There were sizable freedom movements taking place in the subcontinent. The British Empire was coming down. These events caused volatility in the politics of the Indian subcontinent. It deeply affected thinkers, writers, poets, creative people, and politicians of that time and the ones that would come later. This was the time when the progressive writers' movement started. The industrialists, capitalists, and feudal lords were called into question, as were the religious institutions. Many writers and poets at that time and later, such as Faiz Ahmed Faiz, Sahir Ludhyanavi, Habib Jalib, and Ahmed Faraz, were inspired by the movement. Ghani Khan similarly drew his inspiration from the Progressive Writers movement.

The seed of socialism had spread from the Russian Revolution into India, which presented the population with an ideological split. On the one hand, some considered socialism to be anti-religious, going as far as to label it an outright atheist movement. But others, including prominent figures such as Obaidullah Sindhi and Maulana Abul Kalam Azad, saw the movement through the lens of liberation theology. They believed socialism expressed religious teaching, especially its emphasis on helping people experiencing poverty. Colonial European powers throughout the third world recognized the rising support for socialism as an existential threat to their empires. To combat this threat, these powers exploited the religion and used it to their advantage. In pre-partition India, the British bribed influential tribe members and *mullahs* (religious priests) with money, land, and power to use religious sentiments against the socialist movement.

In NWFP (Northwest Frontier Province, now known as KPK) in 1929, Bacha Khan started his *Khudai Khidmatgar* (Servants of God) anticolonial movement founded on a strict philosophy of non-violence. His philosophy was that anyone can commit violence, but only strong people can practice nonviolence, as nonviolence requires courage.

Pashtuns were traditionally known for their bravery and were mostly appointed to positions in the army under British rule involving guns. However, Bacha Khan envisioned replacing every weapon with a pen in a Pashtun's hand. He promoted education with as much vigour as his philosophy of nonviolence. Under British rule, in KPK, the children in villages and rural areas were deprived of educational opportunities due to remoteness and lack of resources.

With the help of some supporters, Bacha
Khan took it upon himself to bring education to
his people. Through years of rigorous effort in
reaching remote areas, finding resources, and
overcoming immense opposition from locals
and authorities, he established 134 schools in
various villages in KPK called *Azad* (free of any
binding) schools. These were basic schools to
make education easy and accessible for children.
Despite having the resources to send his
children to more reputable and well-established
schools, Bacha Khan chose to admit his children
to his own *Azad* schools. This decision stemmed
from his commitment to equality and fairness.
He did not want any Pashtun to feel his sons
were receiving preferential treatment or
privilege, demonstrating his dedication to
providing equal educational opportunities for
all.

The British sought to sabotage the *Azad*
schools, fearing Pashtun education would only

further mobilize anti-colonial efforts. They used the regional feudal lords and *Mullahs* (religious priests) to spread propaganda against *Azad* schools and the more significant socialist movement. The *Mullahs* began to preach that the education provided in these schools was un-Islamic. While this tactic was aimed at the common people, the progressive thinkers and anti-colonial activists saw through the corruption and continued their support of the *Azad* schools.

This tumultuous time in the subcontinent, at the height of the independence movement, served as the backdrop for Ghani Khan's early years. A major theme of Ghani Khan's poetry was to expose religious fraud. He uses the *Mullah* as a satirical figure to represent those who use religion for personal and political gains. His dislike for the *Mullah*, although a small part of Ghani Khan's poetry, made him a target of critics, who labelled him a nonbeliever.

GHANI KHAN'S EDUCATION

After Ghani Khan finished 10th grade at *Azad* schools, his father sent him to the renowned Jamia Millia University in Delhi. During his early days in his village and later in Jamia Millia, he learned Arabic (in which he became fluent) and studied religion and *hadith* (the tradition of the Prophet Muhammad PBUH).

In 1929, he was sent to live with his uncle Dr. Abdul Jabbar Khan in London, England for further education. During his studies there, he had the opportunity to study other religions under the tutelage of esteemed scholars. Eager to learn about different religious ideologies, he studied the Bible and Torah in detail. Ghani Khan later attended Louisiana State University in America for a degree in chemical engineering. He specifically was interested in studying sugar technology which he later used in the Takht Bai sugar mills in KPK in 1933.

Ghani Khan's love for education then took him to India to attend Rabindranath Tagore's University, *Shantiniketan* (meaning "House of Peace"). The famed university focused its education on Tagore's principles of creativity, ecocentrism, and holisticism. Classes were offered in open-air settings under the shade of trees. Courses focused on traditional fine arts, including music, dance, and painting. Here, Ghani Khan cultivated an affinity for painting and sculpture. His hidden creativity started to surface more in the nature-immersive environment of *Shantiniketan*. Ghani Khan's well-rounded personality and intelligence made him popular among his peers. *Shantiniketan* also left Ghani Khan with a great appreciation for the East and the beauty of Eastern cultures. Ghani Khan later built his own house in Charsadda, modelled after the enchanting architecture of *Shantiniketan*, a harmonious blend of Eastern architectural traditions and the surrounding nature. He lovingly named it Darul-Aman, meaning "House of Peace."

GHANI KHAN AND POLITICS

Although Ghani Khan never wanted to be personally involved in politics, upon the insistence of his friends and under Bacha Khan's influence, Ghani Khan came to practical politics in 1945 to represent Pakhtunkhwa and support the cause of the Pashtuns of British India. At that time, three big political parties - the Muslim League, Khaksar, and Hindu Mahasabha, were in opposition to him. He won the central assembly election against all three parties. He became the youngest member of the Legislative Assembly (MLA) from Pakhtunkhwa at that time. He spoke eloquently and had a compelling way of conveying his message. Ghani Khan was greatly hurt by the political violence and punishments that Pashtuns were suffering at the hands of the British at that time. He opposed Bacha Khan's philosophy of non-violence, as Pashtuns were unfairly targeted and, in his opinion, needed to be able to defend themselves.

He rallied together a group of Pashtun youth by the name *Zalmi Pukhtun* (Pashtun youth), to serve Pashtuns in the face of violence. This group gained popularity among Pashtun youth, and thousands became members. His poetry at that time had the tone of a young, enthusiastic worker. The youth recited and sung his poems in their political gatherings:

O' my beloved homeland,
O' My treasure of gems'
In every valley of yours
Are the signs of my bravery

But Ghani Khan was not born a natural politician. He was a nature-loving, sensitive, and straightforward man. Not having his heart in politics and disheartened by injustice, he soon decided to part from politics and never returned to it.

Despite leaving politics, the Government of Pakistan arrested him in 1948 based on his relation to Bacha Khan and kept him in prison until 1954. During these years, he wrote his poetry collection, *Da Panjre Chaghar* (Chirping in the Cage), which is widely considered the best work in his oeuvre.

THE UNTIMELY PASSING OF GHANI KHAN'S MOTHER — A LIFELONG EFFECT

A recurring theme in Ghani Khan's poetry is his relationship with his mother. His mother had passed away suddenly after the influenza pandemic in 1918. Ghani Khan was only five years old at the time of her passing. His poems take on a wistful and loving tone in her remembrance:

Heartbroken when I get,
Grief!!!
When given out of bounds,
The smile of your eyes,
Ever by my side,
And your remembrance,
Takes it all away

He describes a visit to his mother's grave in his book, *Da Ghani Kulyat*, in these words:

"One day, death followed me and took me from my mother's chest to that little mound of dust under which, in a wilderness, my mother's body was lying. I looked around. It was a dry land, with dry grass, red mud and bare stones. There was no flower garden nor any butterflies. In this ocean of hideousness, there was not even a drop of beauty. I stood beside that mound of dust. All there was a broken tombstone and a few other stones. The rest was dry mud. Death also arrived, standing behind me, taller than the sky. I turned my head to the sky and asked the Creator of death:

I was the shine of her heart

Now!!!

In dust is she lying

I look at her tombstone

I look up at the sky

I ask

O' beautiful moon!!!

Can the restless noise inside my heart

Be heard in the grave?

Is the power of death more?

Or the power of love?

LOVE LIFE, ROSHAN GHANI

Ghani Khan's wife, Roshan, was from a Parsi family and was the daughter of Nawab Rustam Jang, a prince of Hyderabad. Ghani Khan saw Roshan for the first time at a friend's house and fell in love with her. His marriage with Roshan Ghani took place after seven years of struggle, as the two families were not in favor of the marriage. With her Parsi origins, the odds were stacked against their union. Despite these oppositions, the two went on to marry. He has praised and appreciated Roshan throughout his poetry. He dedicated his book *Da Panjre Chaghar* to Roshan in the following words:

A dream of a poet,
In the body of a human
Like a soothing music
Coming from the skies
A flower from heaven
In godly persona

A body with warmth

A heart with shine

The grace of Pakhtun

A beauty from Iran

That's how was created

The beloved of Ghani Khan

Roshan was a well-read, learned woman evidenced by the thousands of books in her wedding dowry. Despite leaving behind a life of royalty in Hyderabad, Roshan remained a loving partner and lived with Ghani Khan in his village of Utmanzai in Charsadda. She greatly admired Ghani Khan's creative abilities. Ghani Khan would sometimes write his poetry on scattered pieces of paper, and Roshan would collect them for safekeeping.

Ghani Khan affectionately said in his book, "I'm a brave man, but I couldn't be braver than Roshan." In the following verses, he says about her:

You showed me the Creator

Hidden in secrets of love

My life; you filled

With countless stars

In the music of your beauty, I hear

The melodies of angels

You showed me The Creator

In secrets of love

GHANI KHAN'S POETRY

Ghani Khan had a unique approach to poetry. He did not follow the traditional style of ghazals and poems that was popular at the time. His poetry is mostly in *nazam* style, where a central theme is followed throughout the poem. In *nazam* too, he kept his freestyle. In my opinion, his style of poetry is reflective of his free nature; he didn't see a need to adhere to trends or traditions. His poetry explores love, a quest for beauty, mysticism, humanism, nationalism and philosophy. He is popularly known as "The Mad Philosopher" because of his depth of knowledge, wisdom, and sublime style of poetry. It revolves around respecting the dignity of man and social tolerance. He challenges stereotypes and religious fundamentalism. Religion for him was a matter of personal purification. His works created an awakening of radical tolerance.

He uses several historical figures and events as metaphors in his poetry. Some such examples are *Khayyam* as a drunkard, *Mansoor* as a love symbol, *Bahlol* for his wisdom, *Shirin* and *Farhad*, *Laila* and *Majnoon* for love and dedication, and *Mullah* as a false religious figure.

In Ghani Khan's poetry, the colours of different phases of his life can be seen. There is a phase of young adulthood with enthusiasm, energy, and optimism. There is a phase of politics where he closely observed and suffered injustices. At this time he writes extensively against the exploitation of Pashtuns in fighting wars that are not theirs. In a later phase, his poetry is more nostalgic and reflective of life's sorrows. He was deeply affected by the passing of his only son, soon followed by his wife and his father. This also came at a time when his health was declining.

The Pakistani government ignored his contributions to literature due to political opposition. However, his poetry and art were highly recognized amongst the general population and literary circles. Eventually, with the change in the political landscape, the then-President of Pakistan, Muhammad Zia-ul-Haq, conferred on him the Sitara-i-Imtiaz on 23 March 1980.

Despite the attempts to censor his work and label it as contrary to the established norms and religious values, time has shown the need for such wisdom. His work is consistently cherished across generations in this era of stress, fundamentalism, and division. It has become significantly popular among singers, writers, and composers. Legendary artists have sung his poetry with pride. His work is frequently the subject of discussions and lectures by intellectuals and scholars.

I invite readers to come with me to Ghani Khan's poetry — a world of romance, beauty, humanity and strength.

SELECTED POEMS

1. ON A QUEST

On a summer day,
Like a long winter night
A silence
And stillness all over,
The dove's cooing
And deep silence

Time is still,
On a ride, ready to run,
The world with its ear to heart
Listening to the life and death's account
A subtle smile in the air,
Like Rabab's music in sleep,

And I alone,
Drowned in thoughts
In search of
My dreams
A lost,
Desperate traveller,

On a journey,

Laying on the ground,

But travelling in the sky,

I, with an ear to heart

Searching for a reason for life

Reason for pain and demise,

Seeking,

The bubble of my being in eternity,

Lost in a sea

Of why and what,

On a quest for answers

Seeking,

In a wine cup,

In the book,

On-shelf in a mosque,

Searching for a bond

Among life and death

A stillness all over

And in silence,

I seek,

The reason for rhythm.
In a sitar's song,

In colours all over,
In birds,
I seek the answer for life,
I'm going mad, really mad
Seeking Plato in Tavern?

When I turned my eyes,
To within myself,
I see,
Just an end,
And eternal nothingness,
I'm going mad, really mad
Seeking life in death's eyes,

A day in summer,
Like a long winter night,
A silence,
A stillness all over,
Somewhere far away,
A spark of light
A star?

Or a faraway desert's fire,

Tells me,

In small words,

If the mountain is big,

It has a path to the top,

So, what,

If life is,

A lost moment

Of eternity,

It has,

An eternal beloved to return to,

O' heart, who are you fooling with,

Me or yourself!

To get rid of every tangle

But I must listen to you

For if I don't

I lose my sanity

And I drown deep

In the dark sea of unease

That I'm floating on the surface now

I shall get lost in dark fears

And burn in my own fire
I'll turn into dust while living
And drown in my own blood,

A day in summer,
Like a long winter night,
A silence, a stillness all over,
Somewhere far away,
A spark of light,
A star,
Or a desert fire,
Tells me in little sparks,
If the mountain is big,
There is a path to the top
What if life is
A lost moment of sanity
It has an eternal beloved

2. *DESTINY! MAKE THIS MOMENT LONG*

O' destiny! ease off this moment

Tomorrow, write whatever you like

Put dark freckles on the day's shining face,

Burn fire or shine light where you like,

If bitter you give, happily I'll taste,

But this moment! my love has smiled,

Destiny!!! Be quiet,

Life!!! ease up,

Time!!! pause a little,

For the sake of God,

Make this moment long,

Close your stall,

Shut your eyes,

Break your pen and leave it broken,

Long dark night,

And only few drops of colour

Allow me,

To paint the whole world with it

Allow me,

To make the image of rose
In the autumn's eyes
Like Rabab's music,
In a silent graveyard,

My life, youth and fate, all you take,
But this moment….,
Leave this moment to me,
So, I write in the book of heart,
And make the image of rose,
In the autumn's eyes,

3. *A CHARMING FLOWER*

One day
While passing through a desert
I saw a blooming flower
With vivid, charming colours

I came closer and whispered,
Ah, like me, my friend,
You too, a doomed flower,
Lost from the beloved's lovely locks,

Some delicate fingers;
You won't see reaching
Closer for a touch,
You never shall be kissed
By sweet scarlet lips

It smiled back and said,
Khan!!! Do not be sad,
This dry desert, I won't give,
Over gardens of Iran,

I am the lone one here,
But countless like me are there,

Like a single spark of colour,
I stand in this vast desert

A silent song of beauty,
Like a stunning mark of heaven
Those thousand flowers in your garden,
Like a nameless drop in river

May you too, O' my brother,
Not be dreary in your barren,
Someday, entranced by your charm,
Will come a desperate Ghani Khan,

4. AN OCEAN IN A SINGLE DEW DROP

If the moth is blind,
To the bright sunshine,
Is it guilty if in love?
With little candlelight?

The heart hardly fits
A handful of dust,
How in it I can hold,
The sea of your light?

How can I fit
The earth and the sky,
In such a little corner?
And how can I capture an ocean?
In a single dewdrop

All this and yet,
I'll be held to an account?
This blind king with no sight,
Will be trialled by your might?

O' Beloved,
The creator of Rise and Fall,
O' Creator of birds,
And of beauty and longing,
O' Designer of flowers,
And of the fragrance,
Make me understand,

How can I fit?
The earth and the sky,
In just a little corner?
And how can I capture,
An ocean,
In a single dewdrop?

5. MELODY

I'm an intoxicated madness,
Ready to ride a steed of wind
If one colour is of my beloved's eyes
I fill many dancing colours in them

Why am I created,
I don't know, nor do I gather,
Why I become a passion,
A melody that plays on

To hidden depths of the heart
I enter like a spark
A symphony that's jingling
An intoxication turning stark

Like a fire, in the veins, I flow
An ever-growing flame
I am light that is shining
A bliss, burning with passion

Like air, I am with no existence,
But intoxicating when I am rapturous

In my pleasure is lament
And in my sad eyes are smiles

O' madman, tell me,
Why do you sob when I cry?
When I take a rhythmic stance,
In your blood, then I dance

Am I just an elusive thought?
Or an ever-spreading grace,
An intoxicated steed of wind
Running deep in thought,
Or a melodic prayer,
Reaching the acceptance spot

6. *LIKE A LITTLE CHILD*

Like a little child,
Who picks a basket of roses,
Babbles, jumps and screams,
And throws all his flowers
At the river tides

Standing on the side,
Amused,
As the waves sweep it all,
Clueless of the river's power,
Or the worth of flowers

Just like that,
I threw my life
At the waves of worthless comforts,
And imprisoned myself
Into the Hellfires

Like a little child,
Who picks a basket full of gold
Laughingly in streets he throws,

Bandits yell wah,
You, great son of Arsala Khan*

He doesn't know,
The power of wealth
Or the pains of sorrow,
Just like that, I too,
Threw my life in dust,
And tied myself,
In shackles of distress,

Life is either a lost battle,
Or not enough am I brave,
Not one have I seen,
That is braver than despair

Not yet woken up from sleep,
And the dusk shadows are down,
When I learned the real worth,
Empty was my garden,
Of all the vivid flowers,
Now no colour and no bliss,
No waves or any flowers
Like a dream,

All is over,
Nothing left but life,
Full of longings and despair
My flower garden perished,
My jewels basket emptied
And yet, dear Mullah Jan,
Keeps a chant of the accounts

Life felt as if I was taken,
From one fire to next,
Was that life or a trap?
Where on fire I was set

*Arsala Khan — A historical name, a man in Swabi village in KPK province of Pakistan, who was famous for his helping and giving to others in the form of money, food and more.

7. *A SPRING NIGHT*

One pleasant night in spring
With sparkling stars
And the charming moon in wonder
A madman
Pleaded to his Beloved
Give me light….
For my wisdom
From Your eternal high
Give me rapture
For my eyes from Yours
From Yours only, my Love….
The madman pleaded

With sudden force
A radiance flowed
A trance filled with bliss
The being muted and Rapture spoke,
The madman pleaded.

The madman opened his heart,
And inside could place

Only a spark
The rest was full of his self
And full of the world
And the madman pleaded

The river receded
The beauty and light vanished
And bliss returned to its source
The madman left in despair
It was an enchanting spring night

8. NOT POSSIBLE

When the rage of an ocean,

Comes in a little drop,

And a lament turns

To Rabab's enchanting sound

As if a desert goes,

To the ocean for its joy

And a mirage,

Comes for friendship

To a fountain's bound

Like sorrows,

Become guests at the Joy's house

Or a youthful beauty by self,

Goes to perish in demise,

Or to satiate the Imam's hungry eyes,

To the mosque itself comes,

The Saki*, wine and paradise

As if a firefly,

Falls in love with the sun

Or a flimsy bubble,

Comes to fight a mountain's might,

Much odder is my love,

For you my Beloved,

Like an ocean's storm coming,

In a little dew drop

9. I CAME CLOSER TO MY LOVE

I came closer to my Love,
Only when I am not close anymore,
I heard the beloved's words,
When I can hear them no more

When turned poor, I found the treasure,
Of gems deep inside my heart,
When I gave away my garden
Only then it became mine,
I learned to fly high
When I burnt my wings to fly

In Saki's cup, when I poured,
The hot blood of my youth,
Only then in tavern rose,
The sparks of drunken rapt

With rapturous passion,
I bestowed when my sight,
Only then, and only then
Spoke to me the Beloved's eyes

That who gives his ravish youth,

And turns self to null as dust

O' Madman, only that,

Tastes the honey of sweet lips

10. **LIFE**

I asked the eyes,
What is beauty, what is love,
I asked a pond,
What's an image? What's a mirror?

I asked the fingertips,
What the softness means,
I asked O' drunken eyes,
What's this beauty in a smile?

I said to Zehra*
O' You ignorant of your shine!
Do you know your rapturous beauty?
Do you know your gentle smile?

That ocean of boundless beauty
Answered with deep longing
Life is nothing but a journey
Of losing and of finding self

*Zehra — The name of a star

11. MAJESTY

If I want, I can turn,

Ashes into blissful flowers,

From blood-tinged tears, I can make

Red lips with charming smiles

And melodies from laments

I can drown the autumn's darkness

In the deep ocean of hope,

Precious pearls from empty shells

And a bridge from heavy tides

My soul when goes on hunt

Of the colours and the dreams,

If no light I can find,

I turn darkness into gleams

When the beauty I desire,

In the desert's every grain,

I can make a thousand gardens,

Countless blossoms with colours insane

In yearning if I land,

The springtime bright mornings,

I turn ….,
To sad evenings full of longings,

All a measure of my eyes,
The colour black or if it's white
Day and night nothing more,
But finding, losing of my sight

The bliss and sorrows all,
Just to keep the heart alive,
Tales of Union and the Parting,
All an inner music dance,

When I aim to claim a triumph
From the loss of a fallen knight,
I can make grandiose eyes,
Proud lips and Victor's sight

When I build myself a throne,
From the colours of soft breeze,
I turn a slave's despair,
To a king's luscious joys

My Beloved, your presence,
And your ecstasy is light,

My yearnings mean your love
And my sorrows a delight

Meaningless are Mullah's words
The affair is Yours and mine
This is not a hunger tale,
But of love and breath of life

Covert in my feeble being,
Is the secret of your might,
My frail eyes the teller,
Of your majesty and delight

12. LIFE - ECSTASY IF TAKEN OUT

Ecstasy, if taken out,
Wine turns to bitter water
With no ecstasy and pride,
What would be called a life?

A heart empty of love,
Like a dry withered flower
With love, a spark of light,
Without, like dirt with no delight,

Life with no hardships,
Like bread without salt,
Lips without a smile,
Like a winecup full of dust,

With no trials in youth
Like a sword hidden in sheath,
No sound and no shine,
But a piece of rusted iron

Life, a journey forward
Falling and rising on the way

Some sighs and some melodies

Some sorrows and some joys

Life, a drunken spark,

In the lover's eyes

Life is seeking in the desert

To Beloved's Street a path

13. DUST

No, my friend,
Death is not the end of being
With emptying of the winecup
The rapture doesn't end

By way of dusk comes the night,
Bringing dawn and a new day rise
Light is not without darkness,
Nor is darkness without light

With one, there's the other,
Without the other, there is none,
This strange ocean of being,
It must have an unseen other side,

Thousand mornings of a spring,
Dissolve in a single autumn eve,
Several drums of fragrance,
Hidden in a single basil seed

With the wilting death of single flower,
A full garden is born

Offering all its vivid hues,

Like a gratitude to spring

Why must a world of light perish?

With music turning silent,

Whilst still with drunken eyes,

Beloved's plucking at the sitar strings

In graves are only buried

Hands and feet, lips and fingers,

But who can make a grave?

For the rapture of drunk eyes,

In drunkard's tavern his cup broke,

And the lover in silence rose,

His heart brimming with passion,

To arrive in the Beloved's abode

Saki, with a smile on red lips

Picked another cup,

A new lover, for it reached

To collect gratitude for the Beloved

Mullah, a loser with no zest,

Took his empty cup to grave,

Made of dust, returned to dust,

Dig a grave for him to rest

14. HUMILITY

A man's goodness

When rise high turns to madness,

When ego gets out of self,

Gives space to rapturous bliss

Iron, when fed up with blood

Gets excited with love,

It turns,

To an awestruck sitar string

The time when takes away

A beloved and the love

Only then, upon one dawn

The real worth of self and love

Adam, when lowers self to dust

Endless beauty he creates

But turns into a serpent

When in affluence he sits

O' Beloved! do not tempt me
With your *Hooray and *Ghilman,
For my longing only is for you
And none else, I seek,

Today, in which I walk
With such pleasure and pride
Tomorrow, God only knows
Whose will be this garden

I'm not afraid of death
Because I'm Pashtun
But restless I get
With barren life and useless death

A river full of worries
Flows inside the heart
I wonder when will I see,
A colourful spring of hope

My heart with sadness cries,
My Beloved! when it sees,
The carelessness,
In your lovely eyes

Melody is wailing or a rapture?

I do not know,

Its sound becomes sorrow,

And chirp at other times

*Hooray and *Ghilman — companions in heaven described in religious scripture.

Echoes From The Mountains

15. JOY AND SORROW

The cupbearer,

Holds the wine,

Of the bliss,

And the sorrow,

With empty cup in my hands,

I yearn for your bounty,

O' Saki!

Whichever you desire,

Pour it with a smile,

The rapture or lament,

In my madness

Makes no difference

For my thirst is for your eyes

Fill my cup

With bliss or sorrow

But don't leave me unquenched

In the tavern of your beauty

16. A CANDLE'S FATE

My fate is a candle's fate

Either,

My flame will extinguish

Or I'll burn to my end,

I will sink to the bottom

Or move with the waves

Strange me

On a strange path

Moving in a strange caravan

Taking me

To my destination,

Whether or not

I wish to go

17. O' GOD WHY

O' God!

Why you gave me heart

When you granted me a mind?

Like two arrogant kings

To rule a single reign

Why You created

Royalty and peasantry together,

Like death,

Hidden in every breath,

Why like a sky,

The world is covered in despair

And why?

The joy is scarce

Why You created

The beauty in tender cheeks

Like delicate rose petals

Why do You take away?

Rapture from the blissful wine

Why beauty and colours
You made like two siblings
Why you filled the world
With colours everywhere

Why didn't you send me
Deaf into the world,
Why you made,
The music's sound sweet

hy You gave me the power?
To think and to quest,
And why the power to dream
In bright daylight

Why You gave us,
The wealth of tender youth
And why You created,
The power in hopes

Why you created Heavens,
In the Beloved's eyes
Why is parting made bitter
And union a delight

Why You gave Moon,
The beauty of light
Like a rapturous swing
That swings me in delight

Why You made thorns,
Near the flowers,
Why my heart is made clean
And my body impure

Why did you give me?
The power of saying why
O' God, why,
O' God why, O' God why

18. HEART

Inside my heart,
Is a Hell and Heaven,
Inside it is furry and anger
And kindness and ease,

Inside the heart
Is a sea of joy
And a hell,
Of painful fire,

The heart is full,
Of joyous spring colours,
A spark from which can brighten,
The World with a shine

Inside it is darkness,
Of deep sorrows and pain
A flicker of which can turn
A smiling world to a grave

Full of such courage it is,
With strength,

To pieces it can shred,
The fears of death

The heart, when fills with fear,
Turns frail like a mouse's heart
And frail with fear such,
That a water drop is stronger

When it hardens,
It turns to iron rock
That moves not by countless blows,
Or by pleads for years long

The heart is the path,
The caravan,
The plan,
And the landing place

Inside it is the story
Of reward and torment
Spread inside it,
A world of union and love

This heart is garden and autumn
Nightingale and spring

Inside it are red flowers
And the sound of blue waters

The heart is bitter like poison
And sweeter than honey
Dark like the face of death
And bright like a spring of life

Inside this heart
Is such a rapturous potion
A drop of which can
Enrapture the angels

When it rises high up in goodness
Jibril* is surprised
When it gets into badness
It turns worse than Satan

You created me strange
O' Strange Beloved
Other than you
I have everything in me

I am created full of fire and light
Vast like an ocean and sky

But small, like a drop
And brief, like a moment

O' Creator, for what reason?
All this story of joy and lament
For what purpose?
All this beauty, secrets and longings,

*Jibril — Also known as Gabriel is an angel mentioned in religious scriptures who acts as a messenger between God and humans.

19. MAKAAN* AND LAMAKAAN*

When tired of destiny,
Adam picks sitar
When goes more mad
He picks a sword

Eve, with fears of the end,
Goes to search tomorrow
Gathers colours from the flowers,
And the music tones

It's all Adam's shades,
All marks of his power,
What is earth? What's divine?
Autumn is king and flower slave

Beloved, idol or my Rabb,
All my thirst, all my thought
*Both *Makaan and *Lamakaan,*
All creation of my sight,

Red flowers, white imam
The Beginning and the end,

A flower is the child of dirt,
And autumn hidden in spring

Escape, fear, defeat, all a coward's call
No defeat for daring ones,
A conqueror, forever is
On a journey reaching high,

A flower mixed in the dirt, still a flower,
But called a rose when coloured red
A single moon with a thousand clouds,
Keeps its smile and shine

In the battlefield of love,
A life lost is winning all,
In this bazaar of madmen,
Victory is what's lost

Here, drowned in a little goblet
Is Kaaba's tall minaret,
Here, losing self and finding self,
All a great delight,

This Makan and Lamakaan,

Both creations of my being

Beloved, idol or Rabb*

All virtues of my thirst

All born of my bounds

* *Makaan — The world that we can see,*

**Lamakaan — The world beyond our limits.*

**Rabb — Another word/name used for God*

20. TRAVELLER

The meaning of life is to attain
The height of love
In widespread light of wisdom
That one spark of love

Dusky hues of the evening
Like a potter of love
The quest of longings
Like a trap of love

Love in the candle's heart
A dream of light and burn
And a blind's dream
A hope of light in the dark

In the autumn's despair
A dream of blooming flowers,
In the dark world of demise
The music of the rising sun

Life is nothing but a quest
Of the longings to fulfill,

And to love the unrest,

In the way of longing's quest

Life is like a delicate dream

Of the darkness and light

Man, a traveller

With a home in garden,

But a long desert to cross

21. THE MOON SMILED

The moon smiled and asked,
What are you measuring?
My friend!!!
Love knows no scale

In blooming spring,
Are you counting flowers?
Smile … be rapturous,
And have no worries at all

Your thousand questions,
Have one answer,
To keep weeding
Your garden clean

In the world of hearts,
No room the sanity holds
Like mad *Bahlol,
No weighing of thoughts

In love of the beloved,
Nothing to be measured

And the moon smiled and asked,

What measuring are you doing?

Smile,

For in blooming spring,

Laments hold no place

My friend!

Nothing to measure in love

*Bahlol — A character in Eastern history known for his wisdom

22. *LOVE AND BEAUTY*

One night
The Moon said to twinkling stars
God gifted Adam with love
And us with mere beauty's charm

With a smile, I shall give
All my beauty and shine,
In return one drop if I get,
From his love's ocean divine

Love, the only single truth,
Beauty, a mere shadow of truth
Beauty holds a hasty fall,
Love has youth that never ends

23. THE BEGGAR'S REQUEST

In the eyes of my beloved are
Many beautiful worlds
Take your world back
I have no hunger for your world

Look in the beggar's bowl
Is the crown of Alexander
I am a beggar
Of the bountiful, not misers,

In the name of love,
I beg from you with pride
For I'm your beggar proud,
I ask not with moans and cries

For such ecstasy, I beg,
That won't vanish with death,
Your grief-stricken dusks and dawns,
I never want,

A single spark of moon's light, I beg,
For my beloved's forehead mark

For I'm a beggar of dreams,
And no longing for jewels

If you give me only,
This little world of yours
Then O' Ameer,
Keep your world with You
For I have no hunger for this reward

24. HELL

Whether black or it's white,
That's a measure of Adam's sight
Whether bitter or it's sweet,
All the Adam's tongue's delight

The soft touch of a delicate wrist
That's a scale of the fingertips,
A *Gulanadama and *Shirina,
It's the game of my heart

For some, a single drop of *zam zam
Becomes an ocean of blissful wine
And for some, a soft evening of longing
Becomes an ocean of zam zam

For some, the dim light of candle,
Becomes brighter than sunshine
Some hear Jibril's message
In words from beloved's lips divine

Some find the Beloved's face
In the delicate face of flowers

Others find it hidden,
In the prickly thorns

Rabba, O'my Rab,
My thoughts are driving me crazy
How can I spread anger and fury?
Upon the colours of spring flowers

How can I listen to Mullah?
But ignore the nightingale's sound
How can I wrap the darkness of fears?
Around your beauty and shine

How can I turn a bright morning's smile?
Into somber of dark night
And from the Hell's fury and fire
How do I make your beauty and delight?

How do I accept that you made?
The universe only for this reason,
That Khayyam by force be sent,
To the pilgrimage of Kaaba,

How can I accept that a heart full of bliss?
You made for fears and doubts

And love and beauty You created

For the mere tale of reward and wrath

From Your beauty you created,

A darling and sweetheart

The beauty of the evenings

From the shade of Your tilted lashes, soft,

The vivid colours of your smile,

Birds steal for feathers to shine,

And it's your hand that adds,

The bliss to Khayyam's goblet of wine

So how can I give sorrows to Ghani,

Of doomsday and it's accounts

How can I lay hatred of flowers

In a butterfly's heart?

How can I drown a world of beauty and love?

In a drop of ugly gloom

And how can I turn a candlelight shine

Into lifeless ashes of doom

Rabba O' My Rab,

I am going crazy with these thoughts,

How can I spread anger and fury?

Upon spring and scarlet flowers

*Gulandama and Shirina — Pushto historical/mythical

characters known for their love story

*Zam zam — Holy water from a fountain in Mecca

25. MAN LIKE A SITAR

A man, like a sitar,
A piece of mulberry trunk
And a few metal strings,
Music is it's sound,
But someone else's notes,
Played by someone else

If played by a nightingale,
It brings flowers and spring
When touched by Mansoor's fingers,
A rapturous Cross it becomes,

Man... like a traveller
In another's caravan,
On another's chosen road,
And destination another's,

His destiny,
A thought of someone else,
Day and night only a count
Of his mornings and evenings,

His is only the sight

Flowers and colours are another's

His, are the eyes

Drunkenness is another's

26. INTOXICATION

When I get intoxicated
I go out of self
Like a bird…
That flies out of cage

My joyous heart rises
Above all sorrows
Like a flower
Rising from a grave

My heavy body
My powerless self
I leave on Earth
I mount the stallion
Of my thoughts
And up I go
On a voyage

I ride high
To the seventh sky
Searching…

The spring of life
And core of light

Not in need,
Of Saki's high,
But to find the path
For the mind's ride

My madness,
Love, beauty and beloved,
All a feast
For my stallion's charm,

When I kiss my beloved's eyes,
That's a stroke on the back,
For a flight high

My drunken eyes
When turn red
My wine goblet fills
With colours of twilight

What a leisured life
You lived O' Mullah

You never felt the burn
Of the fire of quest
On the path of yearnings

Your worship is a measure
Of *Hooray in Heaven
You never have tasted
The sweetness of longing
You have not known
Melting in fire like a candle,

Your mind never is conquered
By the ecstasy of heart
You couldn't ever turn
To autumn-stricken garden

Life came to end,
His quest ended,
The madman took
His weary self to grave,

Like a flower
A glimpse of color
He brought to the world,
Like a river his waves
Took him to ocean

*Hooray — Plural of Hoor in Pashto, meaning virgins
of Paradise as described in religious scriptures.

27. *FIRE*

My mud when kneaded into clay,

It was baked in such fire,

A fire that if I don't extinguish, I burn,

If smothered, it fires up more,

Lord made me from His light,

But a speck of Satan added

The closer I got to Him,

The bigger became the veil,

To paradise when I aimed,

Hell opened its door wide

When closer to hell I came,

O' my child!! A voice cried

May you vanish O' inner fire,

Life's colours you ravaged all

Darkness gives birth to light

Like Adam to Eve in rapturous delight

Death when goes in search of life,
It gives birth to breath to make a life,
Tears when turn red, become wine,
Sorrows when grow old, turn to joy.

28. O' MULLAH! YOUR HEART IS FULL OF SELF

Your heart is full of self
And no room left for the Beloved

You are full of goodness such
Like a city full of dead

Your lips are never free
Of the Beloved's praise

But in your mirror, you cannot see
The beauty of Beloved,

Your blind eyes only see
Badness in others and good in self

In the streets of your Beloved
You tell stories of your own shine

Such excited by your self-praise
Like Pharaoh by his power

Your crafty deeds surround you such,
Like a wall of darkness standing tall

When badness in others you see
Your heart gets full of sadistic pleasure

Other's beauty you think is stolen
From the darkness of your beauty

Your blind eyes only see
Badness in others and good in self

29. O' MULLAH- YOU AND I

My sins make me remember Him
And your good deeds make you forget Him

He is the crown of my ecstasy
You made Him mark of your folly

I made Him a wise Lord of world
You made Him ignorant and thoughtless

I turned Him into love and bliss
You sold His name for your gains

I made Him a sea of beauty
You made Him a power fond of ruling

Now tell me O' Mullah
He loves me more or you?

30. QUESTION OR ANSWER

O' Mullah,

Is life a question or an answer?

Is life a union or a madness for beloved?

Is it comfort or unrest?

*Is life *Imam or it's *Gulfam*

Is it the pulpit or the holy arch of a mosque?

Or in the world of bliss,

*It's an elusive vivid dream of a *mirage*

Or it's winning a moment of light

From the darkness of world such large

Is life a question or an answer?

Tell me O' Mullah

Is life Pharaoh and his pride

Or a madness and a bliss

Is it Namrood's golden throne?

Or the blissful departure of Mansoor

Is it the smile of Hussain?

Or it is the pride of Yazeed?

Is it an ever-blooming spring?

Or a rose hidden from the autumn's strike

Tell me O' Mullah

Life is a blissful goblet of wine,

And the drunk face of Khayyam,

Or a broken bowl of sorrows

A colourful garden of flowers

Or the wise face of *Bahlol

Is it an escape?

A runaway from self

Or an enclosure of fire and thorns

Life is question or answer,

Tell me O' Mullah

Is life an ever-spreading charm

Or a beauty withering to dust

Is it music lamenting its demise?

Or a fire burning bright

Is there a resting place for this journey?

Or it's a breath escaping from a breath

Is it like pitchers of *arat

One filling, other emptying

Or an ever-spreading light

Unaware of its worth

Is life a question or an answer?

Tell me O' Mullah

31. IMAGINATION

I'm creating,
A beloved for my heart
The eyes I adorn,
And the lips I kiss,

In the string of countless sorrows,
I'm putting beads of light,
In my pitcher of bliss
Much rapture remains,
And with both hands, I drink
From this wine of delight

With your generous hands,
You bestowed me such height,
Like a drop that I am
But hold oceans inside

You took my wealth and might,
And gave the power to think instead,
In your gifted storm of bliss
The hunger and greed all fled

But hidden in a corner,
A sorrow somewhere left,
That slowly crawled to heart,
Like a serpent from its nest

O' king of jewels and bliss,
I'm grateful what you grant,
Be it grief or even death,
Joyously I accept
The light of your endless bliss,
I carry in my heart,
In the dark fort of this life,
My dreams it lits up bright

They say Ghani went old,
His madness wearied off
And I in my intoxication
Putting flowers in Beloved's locks.

O' doom, stay away,
No time I hold for you,
My wine still is full of rapture
And I pour my goblet full

32. *CARAVAN IS LEAVING*

Life and calm,
Like fire and water
Never will come closer together,
Nor they can

Darkness and light
Born of each other
Time will pass
The way it's passing

Like a river,
Life too, follows a path,
High in mountains,
At times, lower down in plains,

Man is strange,
And created strange
Living in dust
But place in the sky

My love!
Turn your sullen eyes to me

Forget the darkness of dusk,
Listen to tale,
The shining moon is telling

O' lovers!
A few moments
Is bloom of youth,
Rack up the beauty,
Of such precious moments

Fill your goblets,
Relish the hearts
The bells are ringing,
Caravan is leaving

Bring your lips
To lips in passion
The Dawn is breaking,
Parting is nearing

33. CREATION

I made my music,

From my dreams

From my sorrows

From my joys,

With my rhythm

And my symphony,

I made my beloved,

From my longings,

From the colours of my dreams,

From the flowers in spring,

From the autumn's colours,

I created my sorrows,

From the smiles and joys,

From the Union and bliss

From spring and bird songs

I made my life,

From hopes and light

From darkness and troubles,

From worries and fears

And I created my demise,

From life and pleasure,

From flowers in spring

From jewels and the charm of youth

34. TRUTH

When I have no garden
What does the spring mean?
If not in beloved's eyes,
What does the drunkenness mean?

If not from the mouth,
Of a nightingale
What the sweetness
Of chirping mean?

If not covered with Allah's Noor,
What does the Kaaba minaret mean?
A graveyard of the dead,
Better than a city of foolish beings,

If it cannot heal
My beloved's aching wounds,
O' Mullah of what use,
Is your tale of heavens and hell

If it cannot play
My love song,

What does a sitar mean?
When made out of gold

My beloved's tresses if I have,
O' *Zahid!
What is the use
Of your string of beads?

If it cannot hold
The flag of the nation
What a fort,
Of a mountain height means?

A rough path is better
When it goes to beloved's abode
When it goes to *Raqeeb's palace
Then what a smooth path means?

*Zahid — A pious worshiper
*Raqeeb — A term used for a rival in love

35. IN THE CANDLELIGHT CAME THE MORNING SHINE

It is afternoon now
The mid-day heat is gone
The air is cold
Like the winter breeze

The eyes are brighter
But the heart less joyous
The beloved's face says,
The moment of parting is near

The Music's rhythm
Now much quieter
Flags of sanity are raised
On the house of madness

The twilight colours
Took the darker tone
The king is soon to be exiled
From his ruling throne

Sitar plays not anymore,
The evening's sweet melodies,
And the drunkard's rapture,
Left home in *Khayyam's eyes

The dancer's steps are there
But no rhythm anymore
*Bilal's calling is there
But Bilal, not anymore

The wine in the cup,
Drop by drop becoming less
Spring is departing
And roses getting sparse

The candlelight is getting covered
By the morning shine
To the nightingale's garden
Came the valiant noise

To blossoming flower buds
The autumn's signs came
The rapture is all gone
And yearnings now remain

Echoes From The Mountains

The morning stars came up

The moon is gone

Parting moments here

The union is gone

36. *PUNISHMENT AND REWARD*

O' God, I do not understand
Your punishment and reward
A smile or lament,
For you are all alike

Some give a charming youth
For the beloved's forehead *Khaal
Some drown in greed for wealth,
And from others they suck all

If it's Zehra or the Devil,
Your moon smiles at both
O' God!
I do not understand
Your punishment and reward

Some drown with their eyes shut
In the deep ocean of pride
Some sit on a throne
Like Pharaoh with delight

Some like beggars lie in dirt
Recounting the tales of *Mount Toor

Some smile with endless pleasure
Satiated on another's blood
Some happily give life in love
The blind destiny cannot part
A Pharoah from a Musa

O' God!
I do not understand
Your punishment and reward

Strange is the no difference
Of modesty and pride,
Strange is not to tell apart
A*Yazeed from an *Ayaz

Strange is that reward is one
For a falcon and a crow
For You it seems one sound
Whether music or lament

O' God!
I do not understand
Your punishment and reward

A red-eyed falcon on one side,
Grief-stricken in cage
A vulture on the other,
In open playing in pleasure,

Love, pride and bravery,
Slowly wither into dust
Lies, deception and betrayal,
Grow with no fear of just,

What happened to your big promise?
Of punishments and fate
To You, O' Lord is one
A smile or lament

* Khaal — A tattoo traditionally put on forehead as a mark of beauty.

(*Yazeed — A historical figure, symbolic of killing for power)

*Ayaz — A historical figure, a symbol of love and equality.

Saza — A Pashto language word for punishment

Jaza — A word used for reward

37. AT HOME

Lord, You are the maker of time,

What can time do to you?

But!

Time is my master

Taking me like a slave

To a place of nothingness

How do I accept

Unfairness, cruelty and pain,

O' God, none of these ugly marks

Look good on your beauty

You are the symbol,

Of a mother's love

And of a sister's fidelity,

How can a deaf and blind?

Hold the power

To count your traits

A mullah, up on the pulpit

When stands in your name

His tongue loaded with poison
And a heart filled with evil

Your wisest with a mask
One colour inside
Show another to the world

You have countless praisers,
Poets and saints,
But the words of real truth,
Are spoken by this one madman,

38. WHAT I BEG

I do not seek your charming lips
Nor your dark long hair locks

I do not crave your swan-like neck
Nor your drunken eyes like daffodils

Your teeth, like gems from another world
Or your red cheeks like pomegranate

Your soft innocent words like music
Nor your stature, tall like a pine tree

But show me only one thing, my Love!
A heart softened with pain like the *Lala flower

Two tears of longing and love
For which I will give up countless gems

*Lala — (Red poppy flower with a black dot in the center. The black dot symbolizes the mark of sorrows on the beautiful face of the flower)

Echoes From The Mountains

39. O' NIGHTINGALE

O' Nightingale,
No words I know,
That I can use,
To praise your charm,

How to hold, Your glory, charm and joy,
In my dust-made lips,
How to shine, the sparkle of gems,
Through the dust,
How to catch the light of moon,
In the trap of words,

How to hold your chant,
In my fingers,
How to place, the river of Noor
In my goblet,

How to trap,
A youthful dream into dust,
How to scale,

The hues of union with the beloved

How to hold,

The shine in my beloved's eyes

How to tie,

The moonlight in a bundle

Like an eager slave,

In a Sultan's *Darbar,

I stand amazed at your charm,

My bounds I confess O' Nightingale!!

No power I hold to count your delights

But when I hear,

Your message of the new day,

Like a flower,

Gets the call of spring,

The darkness I forget,

A hope for light prevails,

As if in a grave one tastes,

The sweetness of heavenly wine,

Hope awakens,

Life brightens,

And the death's face gets covered,

By the life's colourful shawl

*Darbar — A king's court

40. FIRST GIVE ME EYES THAT CAN SEE YOU

I only know music,
Joy and bliss,
I know *Laila
Or *Ayaz

I know heartbreak,
Fire of Love and the Beloved
I know *Raqeeb
Or *Ghamaz,

To this naive powerless being
You tell your splendour tales,
The Heaven's Stories,
Your glory's tales

Like telling a mouse
The tales of stars
The Dusk's secrets
And stories of moon

I only know a flower,
A garden and wine,
And I know
The autumn and spring

I know melodies and colours
And what I can taste
I know not,
What sin and Satan are,

From this visionless being
You expect Your sight?
From this mindless and lost
You expect reaching to such a height?

O' Lord,
That is unjust
Expecting oranges
From the Babool tree

From this low-sighted
Expecting sighting you
From this motionless,
Expecting a journey to you

First, give me the eyes
That can see You
Then watch me,
Falling in love with You
I know music,
Rhythm and sitar
And a beloved
That I can see with my eyes

I know only love and a smile
And joke and flirt
I know the charming face
And the tattoo on beloved's chin

I know lips
Soft and red,
And the colours of joy
Of the union with beloved

I know begging
To the Beloved
A Saki holding
The goblet of wine

To this crawling insect
The bravery tales?
The tales of rising high,
And beauty and grace,

Why I'll be punished
For lips you made,
If sweeter than honey,
The wine it tastes

Who made those eyes?
That see beauty in awe,
Who brings in flowers?
The heaven's charm

Who made His abode?
Hidden from the World
I drown in a drop
And You, an ocean so vast

I am only a shadow of dark
You, the shine of earth and skies
You a boundless ocean of colour
And I only a drop of joy

You are the life of all lives
And I, a defeated moment of death
You, an ocean of rapture
And I, like a broken goblet

I have pride in your kindness,
So, I beg You,
Listen to a slave's cry,
O' Lord of moon and stars,

I know only music,
Melody and Sitar,
And a beloved
That I can see

*Laila or *Ayaz — Historical figures, both symbolic of love
*Raqeeb — Rival
*Ghamaz — Defamer

Echoes From The Mountains

41. LAMENT

O' shameless sorrows!!
You came when you found me old,
You sneaked in
Like a coward

When my zenith's sun was shining hot,
To ashes, I burnt you
My carefree heart has smothered countless of you
Crushed to nothingness under my elated feet

Now, when my sparkling youth is gone
Your power came alive?
Though life is turned,
Into worries and longings,
I won't fall prey,
To your dark paws

My heart is still filled,
With bright faith in myself,
The charming lips of my hope,
Forever smiles,

As I hold in my heart,

My Beloved's divine shine

My youth's fire may have turned cold,

But still alive are its burning dreams,

To pieces if my heart is broken,

To you, I won't bow

For I'm no coward,

And fears I don't know,

I'm Pashtun,

You might hurt me,

But you never can break me,

Countless sufferings you brought,

But!

My strong mind, you never could get

When you visit me more,

My beloved smiles more

My world gets filled

With colourful flowers,

And a blissful air flows

The shadows of sorrows fade away,

The sweetness in Beloved's eyes when I see,

The darkness lights up,

On the beloved's charming lips

When love tale plays

That is my heaven

Where no sorrows can stay,

The brightness spreads all over

And darkness goes away

*Pashtun — Proud Pathan

42. *A SHADOW OF TIME*

The melody, beat, and charm of this moment
A shadow of time, and colour of thoughts

The camel and caravan, the dawn and dusk
The fingers and lips, and wine and goblet

The night of autumn and dreams of spring
Drunkenness of Majnoon and the goblet of Khayyam,

The power, wealth and shining swords,
Prayer, reward and charming Hoors,

The eyes with life and full of shine,
The lips so delicate, with pride and charm

The fondly looking, and loving gaze,
The slow, delicate, and proud stare

The hide-and-seek of moon through clouds
The image of Ayaz in the daffodil's face

The love so vivid, the beat and rhythm
A shadow of time and colour of thought

Opening of rosebud and the beloved's smile
The beloved's eyes full of love

A sign of bliss and a measure of sorrow
My beloved's red eyes and scarlet lips,

This blissful evening and life's waves
A shadow of time, and colour of thoughts

The place of sorrows, the world of pain
A small candle's light and dark big world

A sound of symphony in a sea of silence
In the kingdom of death like a sound of life

The colours of love, grace and rhythm
Are light and colour in this sea of darkness

*Zamzam — The holy water in Mecca
*Hooray and *Ghilman — The companions in heaven
as promised in religious scripture

43. ISLAM: O' POLITICAL MOMIN

O' lover of Islam

O' Political Momin

Today, you praise Islam

What was the praise yesterday?

The same face of vulture

With new green wings

The Paws of an Eagle

But weak like a bat

Today are promises of paradise

Were yesterday's promises of Hell?

O' Islam lover

O' Political Momin

Your eyes shine on the outside

But dark is your faith inside

Yesterday not able to fight for self

Today you claim a fight for Islam

By trading Pashtun's pride

You seek to win

By spilling my blood,

You try to conquer for others

Like the trader of wine

Who wants to win both Saki and the goblet

O' Islam lover

O' Political Momin

At home you made

A dark trap for Pashtun

In *London for me

You made a new hilaal

From *Balaa

You made *Bilal

O' Islam lover

O' Political Momin

Like a rival's promise,

To win love for me,

A Raven to win a Nightingale

Like autumn promises to make a garden

The servant of the faithless,

Promise to save Islam

O' land of the deaf
O' land of the blind
Look at the wolf
With the sound of porcupine

Today, he gives a call for prayers
Then what was his yesterday's call?
Yesterday's follower of Yazid

Today is named Ayaz
Think more hard,
O' my innocent Pashtun

Learn to tell well apart
Political from a true Momin

Know who like Essa
Goes on the cross
Who in *Namrood's house
Follows the Musa's path

Who in *Raqeeb's palace?
Is calling the name of the beloved
Who has stood up to the world?
To win for the eyes of beloved

Recognize your foes
Recognize Ayaz
O' the land of deaf
O' the land of blind

*This poem is added to highlight how Ghani Khan felt for Pashtuns as they were used for political agenda using the cover of religion.

*Balaa — A witch (left unchanged for poetic flow)

*Bilal — In Muslim religious history, Bilal is known for his specific sweet voice when he would give the call for prayer.

*Hilaal — The crescent/moon

44. *AND YOU NAME IT JIHAD

Dollars in pockets,

Poison in hands,

He tells me to kill a Pashtun brother

And calls it Jihad

That man with the white turban,

And a long beard to show off,

Like a hidden poisonous snake,

Crushing that cursed hypocrite

Is real jehad,

The home and garden,

And creeks and land,

A Pashtun's paradise,

All turned into a desert

That who kills his brother,

No doubt is faithless

That who kills a friend for strangers

No doubt is the Satan's child

The glitter of power took

Your faith and Pashtun pride,

Our Pashtun blood,
Spilled like flowing rivers

Many handsome young ones
Consumed by these dry rocks,
The world is being made,
But our dwellings ruined

Any level badness
Is no match to that pimp
That with the gun in hand
On his way to kill his brother

Fiqh, shariah, pride and else
All ends here
Forbidden is a Pashtun's blood
Spilled by another Pashtun

Get up, you insane,
Stand up for your land
If at all you need to fight,
Then fight for your ancestor's pride

Look at the tears
Of that grief-stricken mother,

And a widowed sister

O' Pashtun with Pashtun blood on hands,

Jump in to protect

*Written in 1994, on Afghan/Taliban jehad when Pashtun land and men were used and encouraged to fight in the name of jehad.

45. WHAT WAS IT?

Was it a smile or lament?
Floating in Maryam's eyes,
When on the cross, she saw,

Essa's blood-soaked locks

What can I say?
If you are Rahim or Rehman?
To dust you turn
The rose's delicate face

Was it bliss or a *Meraaj?
That lit up the whole world
Or it was the river of Noor
In the beloved's eyes

Was it Kufr or faith?
That drove me mad,
Are my sorrows smiling?
Or my rapture lamenting

*Meraaj — meetng with the Beloved
(The prophet PBUH meeting with God)

46. JOKE

I uttered
The name candle,
And You,
Made me into a moth

I intended
To hunt fishlets
You brought me
To face a crocodile

I am a beggar,
I joked,
You made me,
A true beggar

Bravery,
I was mocking,
And You brought,
A battle to my home

O' God,
Much I can't say,
As You get unhappy,

By complaints

But!!!

In truth it seems

O' Lord!

The jokes,

You don't understand

47. BLISS AND SORROWS

Listen to philosophy of madness

From a madman

This is not an ayah

But I have read it in Quran

Life and death are one

Sorrows and bliss are one

Who has seen a death?

When there's no life

The heart is a goblet,

Sorrows and joy are the wine,

Thirsty, will you leave

If to sorrows, you turn it turn upside down

Distinct if both taste

Its drunkenness the same

Both carry a touch

Of the Saki's drunken eyes

In death is hidden
The secret of life,
It's not an ayah, but
I have read it in Quran

48. *THE MEMORY IS HERE*

The eyes are not here
But the memory is here
The king's throne is far
But his killer is here

Long nights of separation
Spent with thoughts of the Beloved
Though union is not,
The longing is here

The sadness in love
As sweet as joy
Richest is the owner of this sadness
With such precious belonging

I, standing with a smile,
In the darkness of night
If the Beloved's arm is not here
Their vigour is here

O' Lord, when you want

To take a madman

You drown him in love

He doesn't have home

He gave all in love

49. DESTINY

When someone asks for pulao,
You give him lentils
Often You entangle
The hunter in his trap

To someone's gold cup
You add dust and sand
To someone you give diamonds
Hidden in a mound of ashes

When one hardship,
One suffers with patience
You bring to him,
An even bigger one

Whatever burden one can take
You keep giving more
How can a Jackal bear
The fear of a lion,
The year
When they pray for rain

That year,
You don't bring them rain

May you not be angered
With this innocent madman
Often, You hit the potter
When his donkey is the target

50. DESTINY- I AM SOFT MUD

I am soft wet mud
In the hands of a potter
Either I will be made into a wine cup
Or a mosque's pitcher

Either a little lamp of a tomb
Or a chandelier of the tavern
Or a broken piece
On a mound of garbage

Youthfulness, life and bliss
Given by someone else
I have no power,
I have no control

O' Pious, in the garden of my beloved
What flower do I call bad
And which one is good

How I become regretful of my sins
How I get tired of my smiles
When the power, fate and planning
All is someone else's

Dream is someone else's
Coming true is someone else's

My sin only is,
That I love flowers
I'm not the creator
Of my sight or the flower

I have no power
Over my drunk eyes
Neither on my thirsty lips
Or my rapturous head

I haven't put
In my beloved's eyes
The springs, the flowers
And the drunkard shades

I haven't made
From my Noor
Music, melody and the beauty,
Of my beloved

I haven't spread

The magical tunes

In the soft rays

Of rising dawn

Who has shown?

*Shirin to *Farhad

Who turned *Mahmood?

Into a beloved of *Ayaz

I do not know who created?

The shine of Zehra,

In the face,

Of a diamond

I am an image painted

By some other hands

I am a powerless, soft mud

In the hands of a potter

I will either be blessed,

Or doomed to hell

Or if both

Then you are Rahman

I can't bear it,

I can't accept it,

That you are the punisher

And a Beloved too

51. DEATH

*Melody is such a sound
That hides the uncovered and uncovers the hidden
From the dark mud, it builds
A minaret so high

On grave it spread,
A precious silken shawl,
To life's moments at hand,
It adds the hidden end

Death is a cover that hides away
The nothingness from Adam's sight
Death is the autumn that takes away
The flowers from a florist

Death is the evidence
Of *Rehman's love
For His beloved man
Death is a promise made with autumn
Of the coming spring

Life is a drop of love in awe
Of the beauty of love
With dark mud it creates
A minaret high

Melody is the youth's arrow at hand,
In the battle with death,
It's the tale of a man's power
Like cannons in a war

That's the tale of an enslaved pride,
And his little power
Not a story of the candle and moth
But of a moth and star

What is the life of Adam
Other than the love of self
Dust is Adam,
And dust is his madness in love

Death is great goodness
You did to Your man
Death brings him to Your home
Or he would be forever with his self

Death is the date
Of the Beloved with His lover
Death is hidden wows
Of the Creator with His Creation

Hidden in death is the other shore
Of the life's flowing river
Death is the sight of a powerless self
That in awe of its own charm

O' Lord of Mysteries!!
And Lord of the darks and shine
Death is the testimony of life
And of Your majesty

*Melody — Known as saaz in Pashto, is used by Ghani Khan for Breath/Life/Soul

*Rehman — Lord, The Gracious, The Merciful

52. *POET AND LAILA*

This life, bliss and my smiles
This youth and vigour are only a few days
The colour of your lips in my eyes
And your presence only a few days

In the end, I must go to that darkness
The darkness from which I came
This youth and the evenings in spring
A melodious moment, a drop of Noor

Your ecstatic smiles in awe
A world of colours, a spark of light
The beauty of your intoxicated eyes
The beauty of your sweet proud lips

The feel of your soft touch
More than the wine and beauty from heaven
The beauty of your eyes and lips
And music and my longing

The morning breeze and the flower buds
And my awestruck rapturous beloved
All a temporary caravan

A story that's told, and soon will be old

This charming image in my thoughts

A poetic verse that's told and forgotten

Laila .....

Take a handful from this flowing ocean of love

Why do you cry?

That you are a goblet and not the ocean

The universe is full of *Noor

My love, you take as much as you can,

Why do you cry?

That you are not the moon or the sun.

*Noor — Divine light

53. *MOON - O' MAD SAKI*

O' Mad Saki,

Of the madman's wine,

Your magical shine,

A rapturous river,

Today I saw in your eyes,

A shadow of sorrow,

A wave of yearning,

A quiet lament,

You remember?

Or have you forgotten?

My youthful days,

Full of madness

You would fire up,

My intoxicated youthful self

Your sparks would steal my sleep

A restless longing would take me away

When you would show up

Like a smiling beloved

My every vein would feel

A flam of madness

I'd sink in longings

And drown in bliss

I would turn to a sitar

With melodies of fire

Your intoxicating bliss,

 Would turn me into a burning fire

You would bring me hopes

And make me blossom

Like a spring garden

But today, you are sad

Pale and in wonder

Your eyes are dull and anxious

You radiate on the world

A sad longing

Like a powerless gardener

On a sombre autumn evening

Today, your light doesn't show

That force and colour

No youthful madness

And no pride of charm

With sad eyes on a journey

You are tired like my heart

Where is your magic?
Where is your wine?
Where is that fire and the red flowers?

My colourful youth, the time stole
My bliss and longings are gone
I was a king, I thought
But I am a slave
A flowing river I was, I thought
But a mud-made goblet I am

Your magical light
The river of ecstasy
Where are your full drums?
Of blissful wine
Why no answer?
Where are you going from me?

Your eyes are sad and in wonder,
You smile but do not say,
"The same moon I am"
But you not young anymore

54. *YOU AND ME*

*Majnoon asked *Laila,
Am I better, or are you?

The butterfly looked at the flower and asked
What does he mean by I and you?

The rose gently smiled and spoke
What it matters if me or you

You are me and I am you
Nothing in me is different from you

Those who see the distinct us
I do not get and so do you,

A madman raised his head and spoke
What is that question to answer?

Sufi tires himself by the useless quest
To turn to someone the best of best

To *Arsh doesn't rise
An empty voice like a donkey's bray

The madman lowered his gaze and saw
Soft, lush grass covering the clay

He then asked O' Lord of souls
Is this good, or am I?

A wave of breeze came rushing through
And kissed the grass and him, too

Madman went mad some more,
He looked up and asked again

You didn't tell me, Lord! and I do not know
What am I? ...... and what are You?

*Laila/Layla and *Majnoon/Majnun — Two lovers
from the 7th century Arab tragic love story.

*Arsh — A word used in scripture for God's throne

55. LOVE

She said,

Love is like a flower,

One moment, it blossoms

And withers in the next,

I said,

Hundreds more flowers are born,

When that one goes to rest,

She said,

Love is like a fire,

It burns to ashes when ignites,

I said,

When the fire blazes,

The world turns warm and so much bright

She spoke,

Love is like a sweet dream

One wakes up, and all is gone

I said,

Life is sweeter than a dream

Waking brings life on

She said,

Love is like a doom,

That takes the lover's sight,

I said,

With no sight, all is seen

But to the world that is blind

She said,

Love is a strange hell

Where the innocent lover burns

I said,

Hellfire is good,

It purifies from sins

She said,

Love is like darkness,

Where one's self is lost and gone,

I said,

Darkness is good,

The ugly world gets covered on

She spoke

O' my sweet beloved,

I wish such wisdom could be mine

Ghani said,
My innocent flower!
Fondly shall I lose
To you all my shine

56. *LIFE - LIKE A RIVER*

My life is a deep river
That slowly flowed into the ocean
A drop lost in the sea
With the hope of shore

The destiny of water
Is to keep flowing
A river doesn't know
Stopping or receding

For the melody of breath
Moving is life, and stopping is death
Every morning is the news
Of the evening coming up

Drown all belongings
In the bliss of eternity
Play your music,
In its boundless depths

Gone is the madman

Drowned in waves of Noor

Like a drop lost in the sea,

In the hope of reaching a shore

57. HUMILITY - WHEN ADAM LOWERS TO DUST

A man's goodness .... when rises high,
It turns to madness,
Ego .... when gets out of self,
Turns to bliss

Iron.... when fed up of blood
Gets excited in love,
It then turns,
To an awestruck string of sitar,

Time .... when takes away
Both love and the beloved,
Only then can one see,
The worth of self and love

Adam .... when lowers to dust,
Endless beauty he creates,
But turns into a serpent
When on affluence, he rests,

O' Beloved! don't you tempt me

With your Hooray,

For I yearn for none,

Other than you,

Today, that I walk in,

With such ecstatic pride,

God knows tomorrow,

To whom this garden will belong

I'm not afraid of death

As I'm a Pashtun,

But displeased, I get

With pointless life and futile death

Inside my heart

A river of worries flows

I wonder when will come

A colourful spring of hope

When my heart see,

The carelessness in your eyes,

With sadness,

It laments

Melody is wailing or a joy,

I do not know,

Its sound becomes music,

And sometimes a chirp,

58. *LOVE - INSANITY*

O' God, I became such insane,
I fell in love with a thought
Now drowning in the ocean,
I fell in love with a pearl

Not able to drink the ocean
I took a handful of water
Not able to love the sunshine,
I fell in love with the moon

What I couldn't place in my chest
I placed in my dreams
To my love, I turned my face,
I fell in love with her beauty mark

This is not elation of youth,
Neither of the wine,
This is falling in love
With the thought of the beloved's eyes

Did I hear Laila's voice?
Or was it Bilal's calling?

Or the jingle of my beloved's anklets,
That I fell in love with its sound

The Moth became rapturous,
With candlelight in the dark,
Or it's I falling in love
With the thought of the beloved's eyes

59. YOU AND ME- OUR FRIENDSHIP

You are the ocean of light
I am a particle of dust
How my friendship,
With You will work?

In the vast desert on a dark night
I call out His name
My Beloved is not there,
Nor are His footmarks

With countless saints, I sat,
All religions I studied
A drop of light I couldn't find,
Just story after story,

Of dust, I am made
To a handful of dust, I will turn
Why was I created?
What was the purpose of this breath?

Make me the love of Your heart,
And for You, I will give my life

Or for this burden of empty life
Find another mule

Call it prayer
Or lament,
I beg in simple words
For no fanciness, I know

You are the ocean of beauty
I'm a dark little speck
How will this friendship
Between You and I work

60. KHAYYAM

O' Khayyam,
You are nothing but lament,
Seeking an escape, a runaway
Your quest,
Only is for Saki and the goblet
And a charming denial

A strange lover you are,
Hopeless and restless
Like a man of the present day
Suffering entrancing sickness
You are a flame of quest,
Of search, and longing
A heart like autumn,
But words like spring,

The surface waves are restless,
But the ocean depth is calm
Like a boat full of flowers,
Only on the surface, you are floating

Man is tomorrow's father,
But yesterday's child too,
He is the goblet and the Saki,
With some gains and some losses

It's a melody playing on,
Reaching its rhythmic heights
Or a drop of colour on escape,
To merge in rainbow colours

Of no value are such sorrows,
That can be drowned in a goblet
The Hope's moon is hidden
Behind the dark fog

Your rapturous mind is covered
By dark fears of demise
The Saki's charm has taken,
The beauty from your heart

You are like a graveyard,
Of yellow and red flowers.

61. THE RAINBOW COLOURS

It's dark, and I am getting lost
I seek the rainbow colours
From the colours of hope, I create
The beauty and union with Beloved

For my ailments, I'm the healer
O' My proud Beloved
Your beauty is the creation,
Of my deep love

When I went on a quest
My destination I found
*When I became thirsty for *Noor*
Saki and the goblet, both I found,

That is I, which becomes
A flower, the light
And a union with Beloved,

In one moment, I become
The fire of your red lips,

In another, I become
Your chin's beauty mark,

My beloved!

You are the creation of my love

Your magnificence, my virtue

But in the dark world of logic

I'm a lost madness,

Like a moon covered in darkness

In darkness and harsh noise,

I am getting lost,

I lost my sight

To see the rainbow colours

*Noor — Light

62. MADMAN

He is building a city
From narrow streets
He has started a thought
From the worries of his heart

He is making a melody
From a touch of rhythm
And a touch of passion and music
He is making Divine love
From the love of his beloved

He is building a house
From the colours of dreams
From the deep darkness
And from the echoing tunnels

And the madman laughs
With eyes full of rapture
Extracting oneness
From the worship of many idols

Sometimes the madman talks
The philosophy of madness

And of the Beloved

Sometimes, the words of pleasure

He talks with sadness

Like spreading the rose petals

To hide the dew drops

He spreads his locks,

To hide the tears in his eyes

63. *A LOST DREAM*

An adorable child,
Perhaps a thought
Or a hangover —!
With a smile, he peeked
Through the darkness
Of eternity

Quietly, he walked towards me
Like the gentle steps of a beloved
Or perhaps!!!
A star was twinkling
Somewhere far through the darkness

In the door of a darkroom
Was standing an angel of light
Deep sorrows in bright eyes
On charming lips, a gentle smile

Was it life moving in eyes?
A thought?
Or a dream dancing,
To its music

Like a little deer,
Walking in the garden,
Frightened,
Not sure of anything
With a hidden dream
Of the desert and jungle

I spread the arms,
Of my love,
Some prayer, some longing
I called ....,
O' beautiful light,
Come and fill my world
With your shine

I will become your body
And my soul covered,
In your beauty,
When my eyes see your face,

My madness, I will add,
To your joy,
To your hopes, I will give
All my dreams

I will make my life
A teller of your tales
My fingers will play
A sitar with your notes

He took one step
Hesitant and anxious
Like a deer from a desert
Frightened in a garden

With my heart in my eyes
Lovingly, I stepped towards him
To a strange world, I entered,
Both lover and beloved I became,

When closer I was getting,
Someone called,
Khan!!
Some friends are here,

I looked back
And the Noor angel was gone
Only darkness was all over
And his was left no sign

O' my little boy
Where would you be
Wondering in a desert
Lost in the dark
When your place is in light

Why have you become
An eternal lost dream
In your beauty is my life
You live in my breath

In one instant, you turned
My colourful garden to a desert
Like a madman, I am searching
A beloved I lost

64. MOTHER - I REMEMBER YOUR DARK EYES

Mother!

Although you are under grave's dust,

I remember your dark eyes

I didn't forget your arms my mother,

That would be around me in my pain

With my cries you would cry,

I remember the swing

That you would swing me in

Your sweet lullaby

That would make my heart light like wind

If you would pretend your anger with me,

I'd cry,

And you would wipe my tears

With your loving hands

I remember your smiling lips

Mother!

I remember one dark night

When my body was burning with heat

With my every groan,

I'd call your name,

You would comfort me with a kiss

With each call

And mother!!!

I remember another day

When our house was,

Trembling with laments,

Your pink cheeks had turned pale,

And your body cold,

With a smile on your face,

You were sleeping,

In tears I was,

Calling your name,

You kept sleeping,

Laying lifeless

Like an autumn-stricken flower

Mother!!!

I kept calling your name,

And you kept sleeping with that smile,

I was crying
And you didn't ask me why
Your body lies hidden in dust
But your dark eyes I still see.

65. *MOTHER - I WAS HER GEM*

I was her gem,

I was the apple of her eye,

I would sleep on her chest,

I was the shine of her heart,

Now!!!

In dust is she lying,

I look at her tombstone,

I look up to the sky,

I ask,

O' beautiful moon!!!

Can the restless noise inside my heart,

Be heard in the grave,

Is the power of death more,

Or the power of love,

How just a handful of dust,

Hides a world of beauty,

How does a single blow of wind?

Change a garden to a desert,

I cannot call the creator cruel

As He is *Rehman

But if death is the ruling master,

Then who am I?

Why is the door of this secret,

Not opened to man?

Why You made me noble of all,

When I am only worthy of dust?

Where is my precious gem?

That, who called me her gem

66. MY BELOVED

Two loving eyes

With countless colours

That filled my world

With endless blossoms

The eyes that made me drunk

With wine from paradise

In dreams came life

And life filled with dreams

You captured the light

From the moon's shine

And spread it

In my way

You showed me the Creator

Hidden in the secrets of love

My life you filled

With countless shining stars

In the music of your beauty, I hear

The melodies of angels

You showed me The Creator

In the secrets of love

67. DREAM

He doesn't know that my thirst
Is not for wine or *Zamzam
Nor for *Hooray or *Ghilman,
Or a fear of fire or dark

The one that burns me
Is my own fire,
Not from Hell, nor from Satan,
That's the fire of a dream
That I am seeking
On the Earth and in the skies,
In the ups and in downs

I did not see, I could not find
Yet lost myself in the quest
In my search, I am alone
With no rival or beloved

Eyes closed or eyes opened
The place of comfort I can't find
My elders made me the *Khan

But I turned myself into,

A roaming wilderness deer

Mullah is talking,

To my body,

Telling tales,

Of the wine, *Hooray and *Ghilman

*Hooray and *Ghilman — The companions promised in Heaven as promised in religious scripture.

*Khan — Landowners/affluent people in villages are known as Khan

68. *MERCHANT*

Strange is this merchant
Sword in hand and Quran on head

*With green *Quba, like imam*
Cunning eyes like Satan

*Heart like *Changez,*
*Trickster like *Haman*

Speaks sweet words like flowers garden
Inside, he stinks like waste that's rotten

He roars like a lion
And growls like a beast

Paws covered in blood
Head up high in the sky

Asking me,
Young man, give me your pride,
Your bravery and courage,

Asking me to leave my pride,
And turn beggar in my own kingdom

Asking me to bow down
Or my world will be made hard

O' Merchant, you have not seen
The might of hot blood

A bowed head is not a fit
For my turban of pride

A throne of gold is nothing
For a free soul dervish

The eyes lowered in shame,
Lose the blissful rapturous hues

*Quba — Green long cover that preacher/Imam wears

*Changez — Pushto word use for Genghis Khan, the funnder of the Mongol empire

*Haman — In religious scripture is a person associated with Pharaoh of the Exodus, an archetype of evil and persecutor of the Jews.

Photos

Ghani Khan

Meeting with Ghani Khan, March 1988

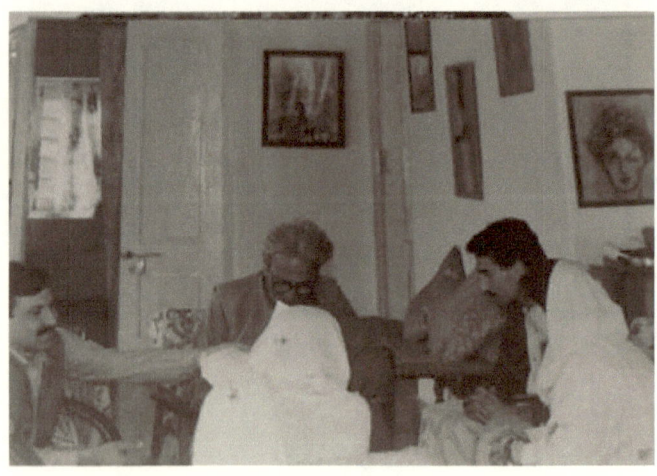

Our interview with Ghani Khan for our medical
college Magazine – March, 1988

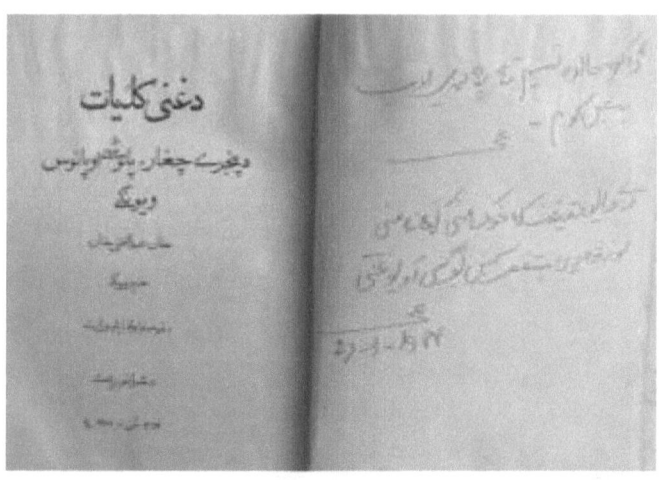

Ghani Khan's autograph when he gifted me his
poetry collection "Da Ghani Kulyat" at the time
of the interview - March, 1988

The door to Ghani
Khan's Hujra

At Ghani Khan's House, when I visited again in October, 2020, after many years

At Ghani Khan's Grave - October, 2020

Entrance to Ghani Khan's house, Darul-Aman

Ghani Khan's paintings and sculptures

Some collection of books in Ghani Khan's

personal library

Bacha Khan with his sons, Wali Khan, Ghani
Khan and Ali Khan

Abdul Ghaffar Khan (Bacha Khan) with students
at one of his Azad schools

Ghani Khan and Roshan Ghani

Ghani Khan and Roshan Ghani

REVIEW BY NAEEM ASHRAF

Echoes from the Mountains is a collection of poems by the late Pashto poet Ghani Khan, translated into English by Dr. Khalida Nasim. As her literary debut, the book is a testament to her strong roots in Khyber Pakhtunkhwa and her deep love of Eastern poetry.

At its core, Pashto poetry is a form of literary art that uses the Pashto language to convey deep feelings, thoughts, and narratives. This poetic tradition holds a significant place in the cultural heritage of the Pashtun people, encapsulating their experiences, values, and aspirations. To trace the history of Pashto poetry, we have to travel back in time by no less than thirteen centuries to meet Amir Kror Suri, who lived in the 8th century. His works are considered some of the first examples of written Pashto poetry. Later, Pir Rokhan (1526–1574) emerged as a prominent figure, establishing his own Sufi school of thought and sharing his beliefs widely. He infused Pashto prose and poetry with a dynamic and influential tone, leaving a significant literary legacy. Love is a universal theme in poetry, and Pashto poetry is no exception. Poets like Rahman Baba have written extensively about the joys and pains of love, using vivid imagery and emotional depth to convey their feelings.

Ghani Khan (1914-1996) was a modern Pashto poet who brought a unique perspective to Pashto literature. His poetry is known for its emotional intensity, lyrical beauty, and thoughtful reflection on contemporary issues. His subjects are numerous and dynamic. If I have to write a few, I would say; the unpredictable course of nature, the wonders of life, the philosophy of happiness and the importance of loving relationships. Besides, Ghani Khan's subjects present an urge to see beauty, peace and justice in the world. Ghani Khan believes that life is very short and insignificant but if we make use of this time and put in our efforts, there is the possibility that our deeds, our creative projects and our contributions to humanity will live forever. He conceives moments of bliss and happiness as gifts of nature that should be prolonged as far as possible. Ghani Khan says:

O' destiny!!! Ease off this moment

Tomorrow, write whatever you like

Put dark freckles on the day's shining face,

Lit fire at some and light another place

If bitter you give, happily I'll taste,

But this moment!! my love has smiled,

Destiny!!! Be quiet,

Life!!! ease up

Time!!! pause a bit

For the sake of God

Make this moment long…

Folk wisdom, life's philosophy and intense human feelings are a hallmark of Ghani Khan's poetry. He professes that there is more pleasure in giving than taking. Distances make the hearts grow fonder. The contrast gives meaning to things. When you give away something, the joy of mere giving is more precious than the thing itself. It is the feeling of losing your wings that creates an urge to fly again with renewed vigor. If you want to have your love in your arms it is not often an easy preposition. It may cost you, your youth or even your life. Ghani Khan speaks of these secrets of life in a poem:

"I came closer to my love,

Only when not closer anymore,

Only then I heard her words,
When I can hear them no more
When turned poor,
I found treasure,
Wonderous gems,
Deep inside my heart,
When I gave away my garden
Only then it became mine,
I learned to fly high
When in fire I burnt my wings to fly"

Life is a journey of finding something and losing another. In this short span of life, one must endeavour to enjoy the present moment and make this short span enjoyable. Before you lose whatever you possess today, it's better to cherish it. In his words:

O' lovers!
Only few moments
The bloom of youth,
Rack up the beauty that one must,
In life's such moments
Fill your goblets,

Relish the hearts

The bells are ringing,

Caravan is leaving

Bring your lips

To lips in passion

The Dawn is breaking,

And parting is nearing

Many poets have defined the meaning of life in their respective ways. Ghani Khan defines life in a very different way in this poem:

The meaning of life is to attain
The height of love
In widespread light of wisdom
That one spark of love
Life is like a delicate dream
Of the darkness and of light
Man, a traveller
With a home in garden,
But a path of long desert to cross

Translating poetry is an arduous work. It needs great courage and consistency to undertake such a venture. On top of that, translating poetry from a native to an international language requires an excellent working knowledge of phrases, idiomatic expressions, and metaphors in both the host and guest languages. Poets like Ameer Khusro, Umar Khayyam, and Ghani Khan frequently use symbols, idioms, and metaphors in their verses. Therefore, it needs a creative translation supplemented by interpretation techniques to translate such poetry without compromising the content. In my opinion, the translator has succeeded well in accomplishing this uphill task. She has done a marvellous job of conveying the beautiful poetry of Ghani Khan to international readers. In this way, she made a creative bridge between Pashtu and English literature. This is her first book of translation. I believe that the English readership will welcome her creation and encourage her to produce more literary masterpieces. I congratulate Dr. Khalida Nasim for presenting a precious literary gift to the world.

~*Naeem Ashraf (Writer, Translator)*

REVIEW BY SKIP MASELLI

Dr. Khalida Nasim's delicate treatment of Ghani Khan's poetry and character conveys both "poet and poems" to the hearts and minds of audiences from all cultures and traditions in Echoes from the Mountains. Her non-deforming approach to translation shows a deep respect for Ghani Khan, a man she's met and adored. I can feel the depth of his reflections as a romantic, a mystic, a philosopher, and a naturalist, with strong hints of both his and Dr. Nasim's Sufi influences. Preserving the depth of Ghani Khan's poetry from Pashto to English is not for the faint of heart…but in this case, it's all heart!

~Skip Maselli, author of "A Sparrow Who Ate the Universe" and "Twenty-five Words Toward the Truth #25wtT"

REFERENCES

1. Ghani Khan – Jwand au Zamana
   The Book, authored by Prof. Dr. Sayed Wiqar Ali Shah dedicated to Abdul Ghani Khan's political life, University Book Agency Bazar- Danishkda Publications

2. My Life and Struggles, autobiography by Bacha Khan, Translated by Imtiaz Ahmad Sahibzada, Folio books, Canal Bank Road, Lahore

3. Ghani Khan interview- Youtube.com

4. Facts are facts- The untold story of India's partition. Book By Abdul Wali Khan

5. Da Husan Safar – Book, authored by Professor Tasbihullah, University publishers, Peshawar.

6. Latoon – Ghani Khan's poetry collection, Book by Muhammad Zubair Hasrat.